MW00892312

MONICA WELLINGTON

Colors for Zena

DIAL BOOKS FOR YOUNG READERS   An imprint of Penguin Group (USA) Inc.

For my mother, my sister, and my daughter—
my three primary colors
—M.W.

DIAL BOOKS FOR YOUNG READERS * A division of Penguin Young Readers Group

PUBLISHED BY THE PENGUIN GROUP * Penguin Group (USA) Inc., 375 Hudson Street, New York, NY 10014,
U.S.A. * Penguin Group (Canada), 90 Eglinton Avenue East, Suite 700, Toronto, Ontario, Canada M4P
2Y3 (a division of Pearson Penguin Canada Inc.) * Penguin Books Ltd, 80 Strand, London WC2R 0RL,
England * Penguin Ireland, 25 St. Stephen's Green, Dublin 2, Ireland (a division of Penguin Books
Ltd) * Penguin Group (Australia), 707 Collins Street, Melbourne, Victoria 3008, Australia (a division of
Pearson Australia Group Pty Ltd) * Penguin Books India Pvt Ltd, 11 Community Centre, Panchsheel Park,
New Delhi-110 017, India * Penguin Group (NZ), 67 Apollo Drive, Rosedale, Auckland 0632, New Zealand
(a division of Pearson New Zealand Ltd) * Penguin Books, Rosebank Office Park, 181 Jan Smuts Avenue,
Parktown North 2193, South Africa * Penguin China, B7 Jaiming Center, 27 East Third Ring Road North,
Chaoyang District, Beijing 100020, China * Penguin Books Ltd, Registered Offices: 80 Strand, London
WC2R 0RL, England

Designed by Jason Henry * Text set in VAG Rounded
Manufactured in China on acid-free paper
10 9 8 7 6 5 4 3 2 1

LIBRARY OF CONGRESS CATALOGING-IN-PUBLICATION DATA
Wellington, Monica. * Colors for Zena/by Monica Wellington. * p. cm.
Summary: A young girl learns how a rainbow of colors can be
made from just three primary colors. * ISBN 978-0-8037-3743-3
(hardcover) * [1. Color—Fiction.] I. Title. * PZ7.W4576Co 2013
[L]—dc20   2012017537

The artwork for this book was created using gouache paints.

"**W**here did all the colors go?" Zena and her dog run outside to look for them.

Zena sees a yellow school bus and a yellow taxi.
She sees yellow buildings.

"I love yellow!" she says.

The Little Red Art Store

OPEN

Zena turns the corner. She sees a red fire truck.
She sees red polka dots.

"I love red!" she says.

"Yellow and red are great," says Zena, "but I want more colors."
"I am yellow and red mixed together," roars the lion.

"I am ORANGE."

"Wonderful!" says Zena. "Come with us."

They continue on their way across a bridge.
Zena sees the blue stream.

She sees the blue sky.
"I love blue!" she says.

"Oh, I see yellow again!" Zena runs along the path.
She sees a yellow butterfly.

"Yellow is sunny," she says.

"The world looks brighter," says Zena, "but I still want more colors!"
"I am blue and yellow mixed together," croaks the frog.

"I am GREEN."

"Fantastic!" says Zena. "Come with us."

They enter the castle courtyard.
Zena sees brilliant red flowers.

"Red is exciting!" she says.

They climb the tower. Zena sees a blue bird
and the blue sky.

"Blue is heavenly," she says.

"I see beautiful colors," says Zena, "but I still want more."
"I am red and blue mixed together," rumbles the dragon.

"I am PURPLE."
"Splendid!" says Zena. "Come, everyone!"

"Look!" she says to the orange lion and
the green frog and the purple dragon.

They all see the yellow, red, and blue paint.

"We have everything we need," says Zena.

"Let's begin!"

What happiness it is to paint!
They work hard and make a beautiful picture

with all the colors in the world.
"Magnificent!" says Zena.

Zena and the lion and the frog and the dragon

"Let's begin!"

What happiness it is to paint!
They work hard and make a beautiful picture

with all the colors in the world.
"Magnificent!" says Zena.

Zena and the lion and the frog and the dragon

and her dog will dream of colors till morning.

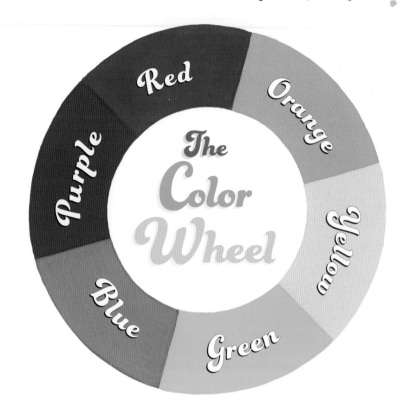

The Color Wheel

Red — Orange — Yellow — Green — Blue — Purple

The color wheel arranges the colors of the spectrum in a circle to show how they are related. Red, blue, and yellow are called "primary colors." They cannot be mixed from any other color, and when they are mixed together they make new colors. Orange, green, and purple are called "secondary colors." They are made by mixing together two primary colors.

· · · · · · · · · · Activities with Color · · · · · · · · · ·

Children will have fun discovering for them-selves how colors mix together to make new colors. Finger paints make it easier for children too young to hold and control a paint-brush. You will need finger paints in the three primary colors and several big pieces of finger-painting paper (smooth and slippery). Note for adults: Spread out newspaper on the floor or table where you are working.

On one side of the paper put a blob of yellow paint. On the other side put a blob of red paint. Put one hand in each and move them toward each other and mix them together in the middle. What color are you making? Are there some places where the color is lighter or darker, more yellow, more red, different shades of orange?

Try again with another piece of paper. This time use a blob of blue paint with one hand and yellow paint with the other hand. On a third piece of paper, try with a blob of red paint and blue paint. What colors do each of these make?

On a new piece of paper try putting blobs of each of the primary colors. Take turns mixing these colors together in the middle. See if you can make all the colors you made before, and maybe even some new ones.

Children can also do this project with a friend. Each child puts his/her hands in the colors and then they mix their hands together in the middle.

For children who are a little bit older, try mixing colors with watercolors and brushes. If you use good thick "artist" paper, use lots of water with your paint and move the colors around together on the paper to mix lots of colors.